WALDEN LANE

SADDLEBACK
EDUCATIONAL PUBLISHING
www.sdlback.com

ISBN-13: 978-1-68021-373-7
ISBN-10: 1-68021-373-3
eBook: 978-1-63078-588-8

Printed in Malaysia

21 20 19 18 17   1 2 3 4 5

SHADY NEIGHBORS

EVAN JACOBS

Crazy Neighbors

Clark's next-door neighbors trim their shrubs to look like dolphins!

Everyone on Doug's street owns an RV.

Mrs. Moore grew up in a funky purple house.

David Albert still watches *Power Rangers*.

Chapter 1
Welcome

Let's bring those cookies over." Marlon's dad smiled. He crossed the living room. As he did, he turned off the TV.

Marlon's mom walked out of the kitchen. She was holding a plate of freshly baked cookies. They were covered in plastic wrap.

Marlon eyed her from the couch. He was holding his tablet. Normally he would have grabbed some cookies. But not today. His mom had made them for someone else.

New neighbors had moved in across the street. The cookies were for them.

Marlon didn't know much about the new people. But they did drive a big white truck.

"Come on, Marlon," his mom said.

His dad opened the front door.

Marlon's parents wore jeans and T-shirts. For "older" folks, he thought they dressed pretty cool. Marlon wore shorts and a T-shirt. His shirt said "I logged out for this?" on the front.

Marlon was into video games. Technology was an obsession. He also loved movies.

His mom was an elementary school teacher. Marlon's dad worked for the city. He helped to plan Walden Lane. That's where the Moore family lived.

Walden Lane was a mid-sized city. There were parks and neighborhoods. The city was surrounded by hills and trails. People liked to be outside.

Marlon had a sister. Her name was Ashley. She was a straight-A student. Ashley ran track for the high school. She was also in many school clubs.

"Why do I have to go?" he asked.

Marlon was focused on his tablet. He was reading a story. It was about a family. They robbed banks. The family had robbed over 50 banks. They didn't get caught for a long time. The best part was where they lived. It was in a city just like Walden Lane.

"Because we're a family," his dad said. "And we're going to welcome these new people as a family."

"Ashley doesn't have to go." Marlon

put down his tablet. He got up from the couch.

"That's because she's at track practice," his mom said.

The house was a fixer upper. It needed new paint. There was termite damage. The old window frames looked rusty. The yard was a tangle of weeds. It was not a pretty sight.

His dad knocked on the door. "They got a bargain here," his dad said. "It just needs a little love. This side of the street is great. There's nobody behind you."

"They're not home," Marlon said.

"That's odd," his mom said. "Their truck is here."

"Maybe they have another car," his dad said.

"I haven't seen one," said Mrs. Moore.

Marlon eyed the white pickup. It was old. The paint was fading. There were some boxes in the back. He hadn't seen anyone, just this old truck. The people were never around.

"Maybe these guys are aliens," Marlon said.

"Shhh!" his mom said.

"Seriously! Maybe they just rented this house. Then they're going to use it to take over Walden Lane."

"Marlon," his mom warned.

His dad knocked on the door again.

Nobody answered.

"I guess they're not home," his dad said.

"We'll try again later." His mom sighed.

"Can I eat the cookies?" Marlon asked.

Chapter 2
Late Night

Marlon was in his room. It was time to sleep. But he wasn't ready. Instead, he was on his tablet. He was lying across his bed.

Marlon was playing *Fight Everyone.* It was a game. The goal was to stop zombies. The problem? Everyone was a zombie. Except Marlon's player.

His room was a good size. It had a TV and video game system. There was also a desk. Marlon had books and a lot of video games.

"Yes!" he said in a low tone.

He had just gotten to level 15. Marlon and Steve McCain were having a contest. Steve was his best friend. Who would get to level 20 first? Marlon hoped he would.

Marlon needed to score like this. Then he would win. He could tell if Steve was online. Right now Steve wasn't logged in. That meant he was probably asleep.

Marlon heard a noise. It was a swishing sound. He ignored it. There were five more levels to get through. He couldn't wait to show Steve.

There was the noise again. And again. Marlon glanced out his bedroom window.

What was it? It wasn't dark. Why? He looked at the time. 11:27 p.m. Normally, it was really dark by now.

The sound didn't stop.

Marlon paused his game. He knew he shouldn't. Not when he was in the zone. Still, he wanted to get a good look outside.

He went to the window.

The white truck was across the street. It was parked in front of the old house. Behind the house Marlon could see light. It was coming from the backyard. The light was bright. It made the sky glow.

"What are they doing?" he asked under his breath.

The swishing sounds continued.

What was happening? Marlon wanted to know. But at the same time, he wanted to play his game.

Marlon snapped some pics with his tablet.

The noise didn't let up.

Swish. Swish. Swish.

Marlon sat back down. He resumed playing.

Marlon was groggy. He opened his eyes. 3:37 a.m. He didn't just wake up. Something woke him up. He heard footsteps. There were loud voices. Marlon couldn't hear the words.

Then he heard a truck's door open.

Marlon went to his window again. He saw two people. The new neighbors? Marlon thought so. One neighbor was older than the other. But they were both adults.

The men loaded some boxes onto their truck.

"I told you to get it," the older one said. His voice sounded grumpy.

"You did not," the younger one replied. His voice sounded snippy.

"You trying to start an argument? It's too early."

Marlon went for his tablet. He heard the truck's engine turn over.

What was happening? Why were these dudes up so late? How come they were arguing? What was inside the boxes?

Marlon finally got his tablet. This time he was going to make a video.

The truck's doors slammed shut. The neighbors were still arguing. Marlon couldn't hear what was said.

He stumbled to the window. But it was too late. The truck had left.

Chapter 3
Proof

See," Marlon said. He shoved the tablet at his mother. "Do you see the light? The house was blocking what they were doing. There was a weird swishing sound."

Marlon's mom shook her head. She was eating breakfast. Marlon's dad had made pancakes. He put down two more plates. Then he sat at the table. Marlon had barely touched his food.

"Let me see that," Ashley said. She sat down.

Ashley was wearing a nice dress. It was blue. She had a Model United Nations presentation later that day.

Ashley took the tablet out of Marlon's hand. She started going through it.

"I don't believe it!" Marlon cried. "We have weird neighbors. They don't answer their door. Then I see them doing shady stuff in their backyard. They were arguing. It was loud. They could've woken up half the neighborhood."

"Well …" His dad put some syrup on his pancakes. "If you had been asleep …"

"Like you were supposed to be," his mom said.

"You guys should be happy I was up."

"Wait, Marlon!" Ashley gasped. "I found something!"

Everybody looked at her.

"Oh, wait," she said. "It's just a streetlight. I guess the light bulb burned out. You'd better call the city, Dad."

Everybody laughed. Marlon took back his tablet.

"Okay," Marlon said. "Just laugh. I'm going to uncover a big crime. And when I do, you're going to be sorry."

It was a little after nine o'clock. Marlon was in his room. He stared out the window. The white truck was gone. Marlon looked at the old house.

"What's going on?" he asked out loud.

Marlon watched a lot of TV and movies. He had seen detectives talk to themselves. It helped them to solve cases. He wanted to go into that house. Too bad he was too scared to go alone.

Marlon stared at the house. He thought about what was going on. Eventually, he fell asleep.

Slam!

Marlon's eyes opened. He looked at his clock. 11:42 p.m.

"I told you not to slam it so hard," the older man said.

"The truck can take it," the younger man said.

Marlon quickly went to his window. This time he had his phone.

The new neighbors walked away from the truck. They were going into the house. Each of them carried two boxes.

Marlon took a burst of pictures.

The neighbors went inside. They shut the door.

Their backyard light came on a few seconds later. After a few moments, the noise started up again.

Swish. Swish. Swish.

Marlon stared out his window. Why was he the only one to hear this?

It was so late. He got his chair and sat. But it wasn't high enough. He couldn't see outside.

"Darn it!" he said under his breath.

Marlon got some books. He put them on the chair. Then he sat on them. He could see out the window now.

The backyard light was still on. The noises continued.

The noisy old truck woke Marlon up. He was sleeping in his chair. It wasn't very comfortable. The books poked his rear.

"Hurry up," the older neighbor said.

"I am," the younger one replied.

The men sounded strange. Marlon didn't like it. They always argued. None of the other neighbors did that. At least not in public.

Marlon took out his phone. He took another burst of pictures.

The two men continued to argue. Then they got into the truck. It sped away.

Marlon looked at the clock. 3:32 a.m. Ugh!

Chapter 4
Sleepover

It was the next morning. Marlon walked up to Steve. He was with Clark Pham and Doug Green. The guys were his crew. They all went to Walden Lane Middle School.

It was time for school to start. Students gathered near the classrooms.

Steve wore a red T-shirt and black jeans. Clark wore skinny jeans. He also wore a plaid shirt. Clark was pretty stylish. Doug loved old rock bands. He wore shorts and a T-shirt showing the Who.

"What's up?" Marlon asked.

"Where were you? Why weren't you at our spot?" Steve asked. He shook his head. His blond hair always got in his eyes.

"I overslept." Marlon yawned. He had barely slept after he saw the neighbors leave. Marlon couldn't stop thinking about them. What were they doing? "I was spying."

"What?" everyone said.

Marlon perked up. He told the guys everything. The weird swishing sounds. The odd hours. The bright light in the backyard. And the fighting.

"And they have these boxes," Marlon said. "They're always taking them in and out. I think they might be burglars. Or maybe killers."

"But you haven't really seen them do anything," Doug said.

"Maybe they're just moving in," Clark said.

"Then how come I've never seen furniture? Why do they come home so late? Why do they leave so early? Why are they always arguing? It's weird."

Marlon showed them the pictures of the house.

"Stalker!" Clark laughed.

"You'd do it too," Marlon said. "What if this was your neighborhood?"

"Hey," Steve said. He was looking at the pictures. "I'm staying over tonight, remember?"

"Oh yeah! Cool. I'd forgotten."

"You think your parents would let us all sleep over?" Clark asked.

"Yeah!" The wheels turned in Marlon's head. "This is awesome. You guys can stay over. See for yourselves. Maybe we'll go over there. Snoop around."

The boys were in Marlon's room. They had set up their sleeping bags and pillows. The guys stared at the old house. Marlon's room was dark. It was a little after 10:00 p.m.

At first, Marlon's parents weren't sure about the sleepover. Marlon begged. He told them his friends never came over anymore. Marlon knew it would work. His parents missed having lots of kids in the house. Having a sleepover would be great. It would remind them of when their kids were younger.

"There's nothing going on," Doug said.

"Let's go over now," Clark said.

"We can't. My parents are still up."

"We have to do something," Steve said.

"Chill. We will," Marlon snapped. "Be patient."

"Great sleepover!" Doug joked.

"They'll be home soon," Marlon said. "I promise."

It was 11:28 p.m. Doug and Clark were sleeping. Marlon and Steve were still up. They were sitting at Marlon's desk.

The neighbors pulled into their driveway.

"They're here," Steve whispered.

Marlon and Steve went to the window.

The two men got out of the truck. They walked into the house. Again, they were carrying boxes. The neighbors didn't speak.

"They've got boxes!" Marlon was so excited. Steve was a witness. Those dudes were shady. Something bad was going on.

"The backyard light will go on now," Marlon said.

But it didn't. There were no swishing sounds.

"That's it?" Steve asked.

Marlon couldn't believe it. His friends would think he'd made it up.

The door to the house opened again. The two men walked out. They still didn't say anything.

Then the neighbors got into their truck. The engine turned over. The truck pulled out of the driveway. Off it went down the street.

What? Marlon could not believe it.

Nothing was the same. They weren't following their pattern.

He looked at Steve.

"I don't think they locked the door," Steve said.

"Let's go over there," Marlon said.

Chapter 5
Trespass #1

Turn the knob," Steve said. They stood in front of the old house. It was cold outside.

Marlon put his hand on the doorknob. It felt icy. He turned it. The door creaked. The light from the moon was bright. It lit up the inside of the house.

Empty! There was nothing there. Just the boxes the men had brought. The carpet was ripped up.

The boys slowly walked across the

room. They noticed the paint on the walls. It was chipping.

The people who had lived here before were elderly. They had sold this home a month ago. Then they had moved to a retirement home.

"Do you want to open the boxes?" Steve asked.

"Let's see what's going on in the backyard," Marlon said.

They moved past the staircase. Then they walked past the kitchen. The cabinets and countertops were old. Talk about a gut job. Good grief!

Next to the kitchen was the living room. Some boxes were stacked there too. There was a sliding glass door. It led outside.

Then they heard something.

Click. Click. Click.

There was a bark.

"Dude," Steve said. "They have a dog!"

The boys quickly looked around. They could hear the dog's paws on the floor.

They ducked into a closet. It smelled like dirty socks. Marlon and Steve didn't care. They shut the door. The boys tried not to breathe.

They heard the dog. It came down the stairs. Then it came into the kitchen. The dog barked a few times.

Marlon and Steve tried to be as still as possible. It seemed like forever.

The dog finally started to move away. The sound of its clicking paws grew faint. Then they heard it go back upstairs.

They waited. Just to be sure.

"Let's get out of here," Steve said.

Marlon slowly opened the closet door.

The boys bolted. They ran toward the front door.

The dog barked again. They heard it moving quickly. It was coming after them!

The boys escaped. They slammed the front door shut. Then they ran across the street. Fresh air had never felt better. They reached Marlon's house.

Suddenly they saw headlights. The white truck was coming down the street!

Marlon and Steve ducked behind a bush.

The truck screeched to a stop.

What a lucky break. They had almost been caught!

"They came home?" Doug asked loudly. The boys were on the floor in Marlon's room.

"Shhh!" Marlon said. "Yes."

"They had a bunch of boxes. The boxes were in the back of their truck," Steve said.

"Maybe they're just moving in," Clark said.

"Then where's the furniture?" Marlon asked. "That house is empty. I'm telling you, they're up to something."

"Are they home now?" Doug asked.

"Yes," Marlon said. "But they will probably leave again soon. Do you want to go over there?"

"Are you crazy?" Steve hissed. "What about the dog?"

The boys stood in the kitchen. The refrigerator was open. Did Mrs. Moore have any meat? They needed something to distract the dog.

"Man," Marlon whispered. "I wish I had a dog right now. Then we'd have dog food."

"Take the baloney," Steve said.

Marlon grabbed the package.

"Marlon?" they heard a voice from upstairs.

It was Marlon's mom!

The boys froze.

They heard footsteps. Mrs. Moore was coming downstairs!

Marlon mouthed the word *pantry*. The kitchen had a walk-in pantry. Its shelves were filled with food and supplies. The boys crammed themselves into it.

Doug went in first. Then Clark and Steve. But there was a problem. The walk-in pantry didn't have a door.

"What are you doing up, Marlon?" his mom asked.

Marlon's mom was standing in the kitchen doorway. She squinted at him. This was good. She was still groggy. No way would she stay up. He hoped.

"I didn't eat a lot tonight," Marlon said. "I was too excited about the sleepover."

This was true. His parents had bought pizzas. Marlon was too busy talking to eat much.

"You didn't wake your friends, right?"

"Nah. They are upstairs. Sleeping." Marlon was glad she hadn't looked in his room.

"And you're choosing baloney over pizza?" She rubbed her eyes.

Marlon had to get his mom upstairs.

They had to stop talking. Or soon she would be wide-awake.

"Yeah." Marlon took out two pieces of bread. He took two slices of baloney. Marlon put the slices between the bread.

"That's it?" she asked. "No mayo?"

"I don't want to eat too much," Marlon said. "I heard it gives you nightmares. If you eat this late …"

Marlon turned off the kitchen light. He took a bite of the sandwich. Marlon's mom followed as he walked upstairs.

"Good night," his mom said. She went back into her room.

"Good night, Mom," Marlon said. "I love you."

"Love you too, honey."

Chapter 6
Trespass #2

We almost got caught," Clark said. The boys were crossing the street.

Walden Lane was quiet at night. It was easy to hear approaching cars.

"Yeah," Steve said. "Why did you talk to her for so long?"

"I don't know," Marlon said. "She kept asking questions. She's my mom."

The boys walked up to the house.

"This place is creepier up close," Doug said.

Marlon turned the doorknob. They walked inside.

There were more boxes. Marlon touched one of them. He started to open it.

The dog barked. It ran toward them. The boys got behind Marlon.

"Give it the food!" Clark said.

Marlon opened the baloney. He threw a few slices onto the floor. For a second, Marlon was nervous. He hoped it would work. The guys had seen this work in the movies. But what if it didn't?

The dog barked a few more times. Then it got to the baloney. It sniffed it. Then the dog started eating.

The boys breathed a sigh of relief.

Steve went over and pet the dog. "This is a Lhasa apso," he said. He ran his hand over the dog's soft fur. "My uncle Richie has one. They're really nice. These dogs just bark a lot."

Clark and Doug looked around.

"This place is really ghetto," Clark said.

"Forget about that." Marlon walked ahead. "Let's see what's in the backyard. We don't want that dog to start barking again."

The boys moved through the house. They got to the sliding glass door. The dog followed them. It started to bark. Marlon gave it a few more slices of baloney.

They went into the backyard. The moon was still bright. It made seeing easy.

The boys saw some portable lights. The lights were off now. They were set up in a circular pattern. There was a blue tarp on the ground.

"Pull it off," Steve said.

"Help me," Marlon replied.

Marlon and Steve grabbed part of the tarp. They threw it back. It revealed a large hole in the ground.

"What are they digging for?" Doug asked.

"Maybe they stole something," Steve said. "This is where they're hiding it."

"Or," Marlon said slowly. "This is for the dead bodies."

"It could also be for a—" Clark started.

"Hey! What are you guys doing here?"

Chapter 7
Sister Act

The boys freaked out. They turned around. Phew! It was only Ashley.

Marlon's sister wore white sweats. Her hoodie was black. "Walden Lane High School" was written on the pocket.

"Ashley," Marlon said.

"You guys are breaking the law," she said.

"You're here too!" Marlon snapped.

"We're all leaving," Ashley ordered. "Now!"

The dog suddenly started to bark.

"You need to give it more baloney," Steve said.

But it didn't want more meat.

Then they heard it. Oh no! The pickup truck! The dog's owners had returned.

"Great," Ashley said. She was so mad. Ashley couldn't believe her brother had done this. First, he broke into the neighbors' house. Now, he was going to get them in trouble.

"Follow me!" Ashley moved to the side of the house.

The boys followed her. There was no gate, just a brick wall. It faced the Moores' house.

"What—" Marlon started to say.

"Shhh!" everyone said.

Marlon was scared. He looked at his friends. They were frightened too. Even Ashley looked intimidated.

Marlon almost lost it. His sister never got rattled.

They heard the neighbors come into the house. Then they heard them moving around. They were headed for the backyard!

"Well," the older one said. "We can finally get to work."

The lights came on. It was so bright!

"Look, I said I was sorry," the younger one said.

"That's all you ever are."

The boys heard laughing.

The swishing noises started.

Why were they digging?

Ashley tapped her brother on the

shoulder. She pointed to the brick wall. The main gas line rose up in front of it. As quietly as she could, Ashley stepped onto the pipe. Then she hopped up. Once on top of the wall, she moved over it. Then she jumped down.

Ashley was very athletic. She was always training. Marlon was floppy. He liked to sit.

Steve quietly followed Ashley. So did Clark and Doug.

Now it was Marlon's turn.

He stepped onto the pipe. Then he tried to pull himself up. The bricks were cold. He couldn't do it. Marlon dropped to the ground.

"Come on!" Ashley whispered. "You're making too much noise."

Marlon wanted to say something. But he didn't. He needed to be quiet.

This time he took a running jump. Somehow he did it! But he had created too much momentum. Marlon fell. He landed with a thud.

"Aahhh!" he screamed.

"Shhh!" everyone said at once.

The gang took off across the street. They reached the Moores'. But then the neighbors' door opened. The kids ducked behind a bush.

Marlon could hear everyone's heavy breathing.

They couldn't go inside all at once. That would wake up his parents. Then they would get it. It would mean big trouble. They had to go slowly.

They stared at the house across the street. The younger man came outside. He looked around.

"It was probably an opossum," he called. "There's no one out here."

Then he went back inside. The door closed with a click.

Chapter 8
Confession

Y ou guys did what?!" Marlon's dad said. He was sitting down. Marlon, Ashley, Steve, Doug, and Clark hovered over him.

Mr. Moore wore workout gear. But it was more for comfort. Saturday mornings were his lazy time. He loved painting. It relaxed him. He'd been on his way to the garage. Marlon's dad was going to work on a landscape.

That's when the kids had stopped him.

It was Ashley's idea. The boys thought it was a bad plan. But she had talked them into it. They were going to confess.

Mrs. Moore had left earlier that morning. She took a writing class at the community college.

"I told you he was going to be mad, Ashley," Marlon said.

"We wanted you to know," Ashley said. "In case they say anything. Or in case something bad is going down."

"Well …" Marlon's dad stood up. "I'm going to say something to them. But first everyone needs to go home. Except for Steve. You stay right here."

Clark and Doug sighed. They were relieved. But also curious. What would happen?

After a group sleepover, they normally

ate a big breakfast. Then everyone would go to the mall. Or they would play arcade games at Penny Penny.

"What do you want us to do?" Marlon asked.

"Wait here," his dad said. "I will come get you. You need to apologize."

"Even me?" Ashley asked.

"Yes," her dad said. "Even you. You guys can't trespass into people's homes. No matter what you think is going on there. It's wrong. We have to live near these people. They're our new neighbors. We want them to know we respect their privacy."

It was an hour later. Marlon's dad hadn't returned. The boys were downstairs. The TV was on.

Ashley had left. She didn't want to. But

she had a track meet. It was at Clover High School. If she missed the bus, she would miss the event.

"What do you think he's doing over there?" Steve asked.

"I don't know," Marlon said.

He was staring out the living room window. Marlon eyed the white truck. Another strange sound came from the old house. It wasn't the swish sound Marlon had heard. It was more like buzzing.

"What if they are holding him as a hostage?" Steve asked.

"I was thinking the same thing," Marlon said. "I don't think my dad brought his phone. Maybe he's tied up. He can't even call for help."

"What if they've turned the house into

a spaceship?" Steve asked. "He could be in a brain-sucking chamber."

Marlon was nervous. What if the buzzing noise wasn't the sound of wood being cut? What if they were cutting up his dad?

"I'm calling the police," Marlon said. He took out his phone.

"What are you going to say?"

An even louder noise suddenly came from the strange house.

Chapter 9
Explosion

What was that?" Marlon asked. The boys stared out the window. Smoke rose from the house.

"Their house is on fire!" Steve said.

The boys ran outside. Other neighbors stood on their front lawns. Marlon dialed 911 on his phone. He kept moving toward the house.

Steve grabbed him. "What are you doing?" he asked. "That place is in flames!"

"My dad's in there!" Marlon yelled. He pulled away from his friend.

Everyone could see the fire. Flames shot through a window. Suddenly the front door burst open.

Where was the fire truck? The house was going to burn down. The whole street could be at risk!

Smoke poured from the open door. Then Marlon's dad came out.

"Dad!" Marlon called.

"Stay away!" Marlon's dad yelled.

Marlon's dad carried something. Behind his dad was the younger neighbor. Then Marlon realized what they were carrying. It was a body. The older man …

They brought him to the sidewalk. Other neighbors rushed over.

The younger man climbed the brick wall. It was the same wall Marlon and his friends had hopped over last night.

"What's he doing?" Marlon asked.

"Is he crazy?" Steve said.

Seconds later he was back over the wall. The dog squirmed in his arms. The neighbor ran back to Marlon's dad.

Marlon heard sirens.

A big fire truck roared up the street. Behind the truck was a police car. An ambulance followed.

In seconds, firefighters battled the flames.

Everyone watched in awe.

It didn't take long before the fire was put out.

Everyone cheered.

Smoke still poured from the house.

EMTs helped the three men. The older man wore an oxygen mask. The emergency workers checked him out.

The entire street was foggy with smoke.

Chapter 10
House Flippers

Firefighters worked on the house. They made sure there were no flames left. The smoke was not as thick now. Neighbors still watched curiously. Others offered to help.

"Let's go talk to my dad," Marlon said.

Marlon and Steve crossed the street.

"Dad," Marlon said. "Are you okay?"

"Marlon." His dad eyed him. "Maybe you should go back across the street."

"I think things are under control," the younger neighbor said. "When I went back inside, I turned off the gas."

The dog barked. The younger neighbor shushed it. He pet its head.

The older man looked at the boys. He took off his oxygen mask.

Marlon started to get nervous. Did he know what they had done?

"So this is Marlon and his friend Steve." The older man smiled.

"Marlon," his dad said. "I think now is a good time to apologize."

All eyes turned to him.

"Sorry about your house," Marlon said. "I mean … sorry for going inside last night. Sorry for spying."

The two neighbors looked at each other.

"Well," the older man said. "I'm Darren

Albert. This is my son, David. He was your age once. David did silly stuff like that too."

David grinned.

"We flip homes. We are working on a big job right now," Mr. Albert said. "It's about 100 miles away. That's why we're always up so early."

"And we're trying to settle in here." David pointed to the house. "So we're moving stuff from the old place. It sold fast. We weren't ready. Everything's in boxes. The furniture is coming last. I guess that's a good thing now."

Marlon looked at Steve. That explained the boxes. It explained the late hours.

But what about the explosion?

Mr. Albert cleared up the mystery. "We're putting in a pool," he said. "That's why we've been digging."

"I accidentally broke the main gas line," David said. "I didn't even realize it."

"We just lit the grill. Then your dad came over," Mr. Albert said.

"And that's when everything went up in flames," Marlon's dad said.

"I'm glad we're all okay," David said.

Everyone agreed with that.

"We want to be done. It's tough working on the flip. Then trying to fix this place …" David said. "It's easier to work on the pool's foundation at night. There's nobody behind us. Sorry if we were loud."

Mr. Albert was a widower. This explained a lot. They weren't the most organized guys.

"Do you have any other questions, Detective Moore?" Marlon's dad joked.

Everyone laughed.

"Well," Marlon said. "Nah, it's fine."

"Go ahead and ask," Mr. Albert said, smiling. "We're neighbors. You may as well get to know us."

"Um …" Marlon said. "Why are you always arguing?"

The Alberts cracked up.

"That's just how we talk." David laughed.

"Yeah," Mr. Albert said. "We're tight, Marlon. When you live together—"

"And work together," David said.

"You're bound to argue." Mr. Albert smiled. "It doesn't really mean anything. You still love each other."

"Yes you do." Mr. Moore squeezed his son's shoulder. "No matter what you do."

"Yeah," Marlon said. He gave his dad a hug. "You're right. Thank you for being so understanding."

The dog barked again. It tried to wiggle out of David's arms.

"Oh yeah," Marlon said. "What's your dog's name?"

Mr. Albert and David looked at the dog. They pet its soft fur.

"Baloney," David said.

Marlon and Steve looked at each other. They cracked up. Tears ran down their faces.

Now they had some more explaining to do!